This book belongs to

· ·

To
Lizzie and
Adrian

MORE AND MORE RABBITS
A RED FOX BOOK 978 0 099 47758 7

First published in Great Britain by Hutchinson,
an imprint of Random House Children's Books

Hutchinson edition published 2006
Red Fox edition published 2007

1 3 5 7 9 10 8 6 4 2

Copyright © Nicholas Allan, 2006

The right of Nicholas Allan to be identified as the author and
illustrator of this work has been asserted in accordance with the
Copyright, Designs and Patents Act 1988. All rights reserved.

Red Fox Books are published by Random House Children's Books,
61–63 Uxbridge Road, London W5 5SA,
a division of The Random House Group Ltd,
London, Sydney, Auckland, Johannesburg, India and agencies throughout the world.

THE RANDOM HOUSE GROUP Limited Reg. No. 954009
www.kidsatrandomhouse.co.uk

A CIP catalogue record for this book is available from the British Library

Printed in China

More and More

Rabbits

Nicholas Allan

RED FOX

Mr and Mrs Tail had . . .

3 little children.

They loved each one but 3 was enough!

Yet when they went to bed at night . . .   it wasn't long before . . .

they had 3 more.

They loved each one but 6 was enough!

"But what is making the babies?"
asked Mr Tail.

So they bought a new bed. Yet when
they went to sleep that night . . .

"It must be . . . the bed," said Mrs Tail.

it wasn't long before they had 3 more.

They loved each one but 9 was enough!

"If it's not the bed it must be . . .

So out went the cat.
Yet when they went to bed that night . . .

the cat!" said Mr Tail.

it wasn't long before they had 3 more.

They loved each one but 12 was enough!

"If it's not the cat, it must be . . . the moon!"
they said. So they drew the curtain and went to bed.

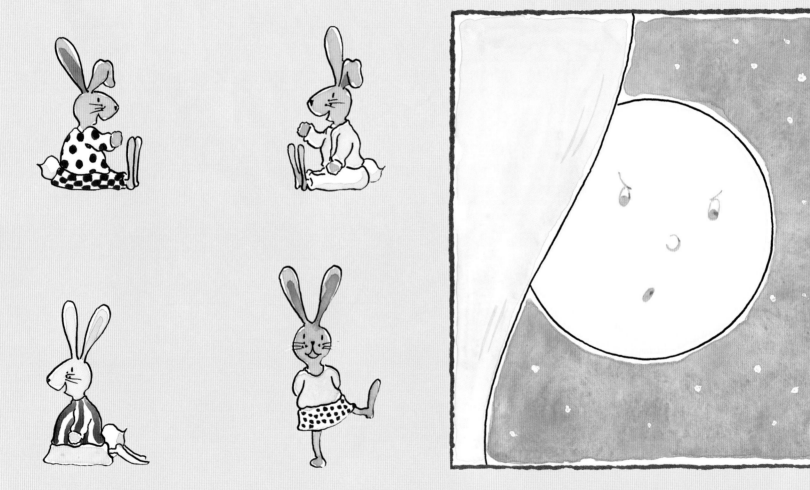

But it wasn't long before they had 3 more.

They loved each and every one but 15 was enough!

"It's not the bed. It's not the cat.
It's not the moon . . .

So Mrs Tail went on Mr Tail's

It must be . . . us!" said Mrs Tail.

side of the bed . . .

and Mr Tail went on Mrs Tail's

side of the bed . . .   But it wasn't long before . . .

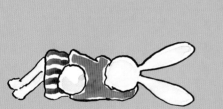

there was no more room left in the house!

So the children slept in Mr and Mrs Tail's bed . . . and Mr and Mrs Tail slept apart on the floor.

And THEN there were no more babies!

But when the children
grew up and went away . . .

So they jumped back into bed

Mr and Mrs Tail grew lonely.
"What shall we do now?" they said.

and it wasn't long before there were . . .

more . . .

and more . . .

and EVEN MORE!

And they loved each
and every one . . .

BUT . . .

enough . . .

was enough!

More books by the brilliant Nicholas Allan . . .

Where Willy Went

The Queen's Knickers

Jesus' Christmas Party

Jesus' Day Off

Cinderella's Bum

The Dove

Heaven